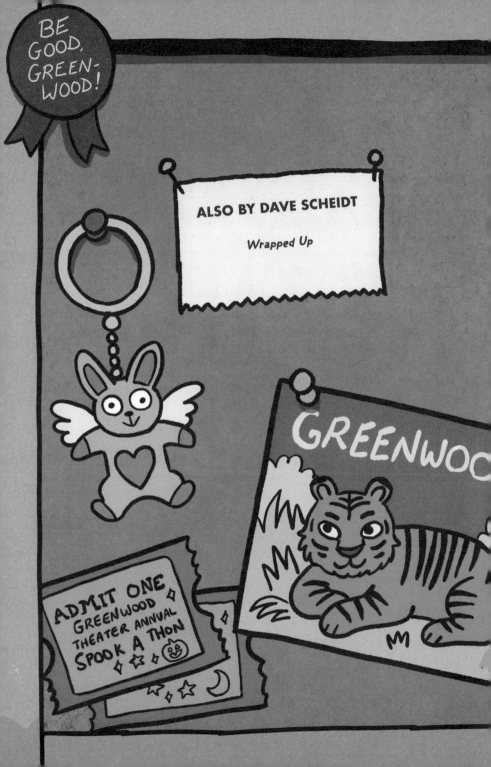

ALSO BY DAVE SCHEIDT

Wrapped Up

MAYOR GOOD BOY

Written by Dave Scheidt
Illustrated by Miranda Harmon

ZOO

VOTE MGB

RH GRAPHIC

NEW YORK

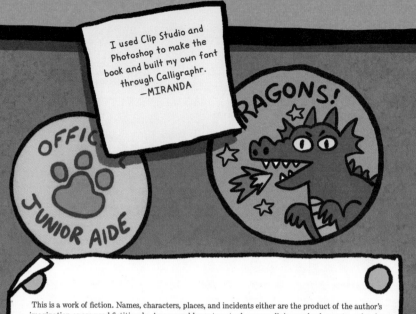

I used Clip Studio and Photoshop to make the book and built my own font through Calligraphr.
—MIRANDA

Text copyright © 2021 by Dave Scheidt
Cover art and interior illustrations copyright © 2021 by Miranda Harmon

All rights reserved. Published in the United States by RH Graphic, an imprint of Random House Children's Books, a division of Penguin Random House LLC, New York.

RH Graphic with the book design is a trademark of Penguin Random House LLC.

Visit us on the web! RHKidsGraphic.com • @RHKidsGraphic

Educators and librarians, for a variety of teaching tools, visit us at RHTeachersLibrarians.com

Library of Congress Cataloging-in-Publication Data is available upon request.
ISBN 978-0-593-12487-1 (hardcover) — ISBN 978-0-593-12537-3 (library binding)
ISBN 978-0-593-12488-8 (ebook)

Designed by Patrick Crotty

MANUFACTURED IN CHINA
10 9 8 7 6 5 4 3 2 1
First Edition

RH GRAPHIC
A comic on every bookshelf.

Dad. Quick. Give me your phone!

Abby! You want to take some weird selfies? Watch this!

Hang on! Something is happening!

The results are in, and boy oh boy, are things about to get weird in Greenwood!

What are they saying?

Who won? It better not be who I think it is!

People of Greenwood! Your new mayor is...

4

Wow. I can't believe he won.

YESSS!!

I'm not going to let some mangy mutt ruin our town!

What's next? We pick a BEETLE as our senator?

Aww! I love bugs!

Can't be any worse than our last mayor!

He smelled like old candy and armpits!

I say we go have a talk with this new mayor of ours and tell him how we feel!

Yeah!

CITY HALL

Uh-oh.

It is my honor to introduce to you my dear friend Mayor Good Boy!

He's even fluffier in real life!

Woo!

Psst, Ms. Monica!

I don't think I can do this!

Get. Out. Here.

We're having a little technical problem. One second, everyone!

YAWN

7

What are we going to do?

THERE HE IS!

Nowhere to run now, little doggie!

Aaron, I can't believe I'm saying this, but can you take off your shoes?

SURE!

FWIP

Now what?

UGH, what's that smell?

It smells like my pep-pep's barn!

It smells like a zombie's gym towel!

Aaron, do me a favor and stand in front of that fan over there.

Man. What is that smell? GROSS!

I'm gonna barf.

HA HA HA HA HA HA

I'm gonna be sick!

EXIT

Need...air...

Ehh, I dunno... I'm not sure I could be much help...

Oh, that is SUCH a good idea, Ms. Monica!

whisper whisper

Excuse me for a second.

YAAAWN

Umm?

ZZZZZ

BORK
BORK BORK

Aren't you forgetting something, Mr. Mayor?

Yeah. Aren't you going to offer us any cheese?

Didn't you have something to ask Abby and Aaron?

HA HA HA

Oh yeah!

Abby and Aaron's house.
The next morning.

THUD

ABBY, WAKE UP!
ABBY! ABBY!

I'M AWAKE!
I'M AWAKE!

Later, skaters!

I'm SO nervous. I feel like I'm gonna barf!

Please don't barf on my tux.

Seriously, though. You got this! Just act casual!

Morning, Abby! Morning, Aaron!

Good morning, Mr. Kupperman!

Morning, Ms. Stanley! Morning, Admiral Meowington!

MROW!

31

Hang in there, man!

FWIIIIT

CLICK

WHOOOSH

THAT WAS THE COOLEST THING I HAVE EVER SEEN IN MY ENTIRE LIFE! ALIENS JUST DESTROYED MY STINKY SOCKS!

CLAP CLAP

33

Hi, Ms. Monica, I'm not sure if you remember me but—

ABBY! AARON!

I wanted to thank you. If it weren't for you two, I don't know what would have happened!

You probably would have died.

HA HA HA! I'm glad we didn't die. That wouldn't have been cool.

Look at you, Aaron! You are KILLING it with that tuxedo!

Told ya!

First of all, thank you SO much for being here!

There is something about you kids... You got something special!

Aww...

What do you mean, "special"? Like if I was born with TWO butts instead of ONE?

Whoa! TWO butts? Now, THAT would be something special!

We got a job for you! Of course, that's if you're up to it!

We'll try our best! Right, Aaron?

Aaron?

Ow!

SLAP

Here's a list of things we need your help taking care of around town. I think you guys will be able to smooth things over with all our constituents.

That sounds amazing and great and everything. I just have one issue.

Shoot.

I don't know what a constituent is.

HA HA HA
HA HA
HA HA
HA

Constituents are all the people in town that I promised to protect and take care of! That we're going to take care of together!

You can count on us, Mayor Good Boy!

I hope...

43

Let me just text Ms. Monica...

AARON, SHE'S RESPONDING! I can't believe I have a real live texting friend now!

SSSIP

Ms. Monica

Yo!

Nice to see you again!

You look like those guys from that movie who get eaten by dinosaurs!

Uh, thanks?

We got you uniforms too! Check it out!

YESSSS!

Maybe a T. rex will eat us now, and then I won't have to go back to school!

This event is a sort of meet and greet called Getting Wild with the Mayor.

We think it'll be a great opportunity for the people of Greenwood to meet Mayor Good Boy while helping the zoo raise some money.

Aww! That is such a good idea! How can we help?

Here's a sign-in sheet. Make sure everyone who shows up signs this!

Oh, and keep an eye out for this weirdo.

You may have seen this grump on election night. He's declared Mayor Good Boy his mortal enemy.

Aren't old people supposed to be kind and smart and give you gross candy?

Not this guy. His name is Mervis Hogpepper. He's started a group called the Anti-Good Boy Society, and he's trying to recruit as many people as possible.

He thinks Mayor Good Boy is going to ruin Greenwood.

SIPPP

So what do you want us to do? Kill him or something?

SPFFFF

That's nice of you to offer your services, Aaron, but that's very illegal.

Just keep an eye out for him. If you see him, let me know.

Look! People are starting to show up!

Mayor Good Boy! You are awfully quiet. Is everything okay?

Of course.

ZZZZZZZZ

If anyone would like to make any donations to the Mayor Good Boy snack fund, please see me.

Hahaha, that is so funny!

Such cute kids!

What a funny joke!

I would NEVER joke about snacks. That's the only thing in life I will ever take seriously.

There we go.

Can I have a six-piece chicken nuggets? I don't need a bag. The less evidence, the better...

FOOD
JUNGLE BURG
DINO NUGGETS
CHEETAH CHILI

RINKS
NOR JUICE
LEPHANT WATER
LAR SLUSH

Hey, you haven't seen any scary old men around here, have you?

That's like eighty percent of our visitors. Have a nice day.

Man. Where is Aaron? He should have been back by now.

Abby, is everything okay?

Yeah, I think Aaron is just getting into trouble somewhere. I'll be right back.

Text me!

Okay!

Ooo OOO Ooo!

Those are MY nuggets, you jerk!

Heh! Not anymore!

Well, I guess that's karma.

CLICK

SHAKE SHAKE

Ugh, so hungry!

GRRROWL

Oook Oook

Why don't you just buy more chicken nuggets?

Dude, I'm eight! I don't have any money!

Plus, stealing is wrong!

I'm coming for ya!

AARON ABLEMAN! GET DOWN HERE RIGHT NOW!

Oh, hey, Abby! I'll be right out. Let me just grab my nuggets.

That's your little brother?

Unfortunately.

Wait till Mom and Dad hear about this!

Oh no! He's freeing the other animals, too!

Oh no! What if they eat all the snacks in the zoo? What then?

We gotta go warn Mayor Good Boy!

RUNNN! WE HAVE TO SAVE THE SNACKS!

Aaron. Whatever you do, don't look back.

We're outside Greenwood Zoo, where less than twelve hours ago, a young boy's gluttonous mistake descended the zoo into utter chaos and released a pack of wild animals upon the citizens of Greenwood.

Steenz Stewart
Monkey Business in Greenwood!

I could see it in his eyes, man. That ape is LUCKY that kid didn't catch him.

The second that chimp yanked that kid's chicken nuggets, darkness filled his eyes.

Did you see what he looked like?

He looked exactly like this.

Thankfully almost all the animals were apprehended last night besides one.

Please be advised that this ape is still on the loose and considered unarmed and extremely into chicken nuggets.

Well, I guess it could have been worse?

CLICK

I guess I don't need my disguise anymore, then? NICE!

You think that just because you got away with it last night makes it okay?

No... but...

You could have gotten yourself hurt or worse!

That was a really bad idea, Aaron.

I'm sorry...

Look, man. I get it. Chicken nuggets are great. They are probably in my top five, but you CANNOT do stuff like that anymore, okay?

I am really, really sorry we let you down, Mayor Good Boy.

I hope we can make it up to you.

I got another job for you guys!

Oh! Oh! Is it a spy mission?

Special Agent Aaron Ableman reporting for duty.

It's actually cooler than that! It's...

A few hours later...

See! Look at that! A real community garden.

What a lightweight!

ZZZZZZ

You guys did an amazing job today. Thank you.

No. Thank you.

Sounds like my parents are here!

Hi, Mr. Mayor!

BEEP BEEP

SKIP SKIP SKIP

ZZZZZ

ZZZZZ

I've seen a lot of mayors come and go here in Greenwood...

And let me tell you, this town has never been this exciting!

He's so polite too! He was here last week and couldn't have been nicer. He was the only one who noticed my new haircut!

Have you seen this? I've been seeing them all over town lately!

12 p.m.

mayor

RING RING RINGGG

Mayor Good Boy's office! This is Abby speaking! How can I help you?

I have a question.

I'd love to help!

Can you send that mutt back to the pound?

CLICK

Who tries to order ten boxes of beef jerky and trail mix? BIGFOOT! That's who!

Psst, Abby.

Is it the Bigfoot guy again? Just tell him we'll send someone out.

We'll send someone out soon, sir.

Can you deal with the aliens, too? Their technology is disrupting my microwave frequencies and not cooking my TV dinners right.

Yes. Of course we'll take care of the aliens, too. See you soon.

How often does that guy call?

CLICK

CRUNCH CRUNCH

Every. Single. Day.

You guys are doing great, by the way. I'm able to get so much work done having you around.

It's been fun. You never know what sort of person is going to call next!

ARE THOSE CHIPS?

RUSTLE RUSTLE

MUNCH MUNCH

RUSTLE RUSTLE

I'll grab this one.

RING RING

Okay. Okay. We'll be right there, ma'am.

We got work to do! Let's do it.

97

Don't worry, little guy! We'll get you down soon! Hold on tight!

Whoa! Is that Mayor Good Boy?

Would it be rude if I pet him?

No need to worry, ma'am. I have a very talented group of friends with me who can help.

I'm too old to try to climb up one of those trees! My husband broke his bottom in the war, so he's no help, either!

Took a grenade to the butt in '68! It's 95% stainless steel now!

WOBBLE
WOBBLE

What's your problem, man? I'm just up here trying to kick it with my bros.

Yeah!

Hey. I feel you. I just think maybe it would be better to find somewhere else to chill.

That old lady threw a shoe at me! Very disrespectful.

It's bad enough that we got that weird kid always trying to hug us! It's like...back off, kid! I don't know you like that!

Wait a second...Mayor Good Boy can speak raccoon?

Ha! I guess so!

Wow. Is there anything Mayor Good Boy can't do?

Dogs can't eat chocolate. They'll die.

Respect.

SHAKE SHAKE

HUG ME!

UH-OH!

MAYOR GOOD BOY, PLEASE SAVE MY GRANDSON!

CRACK!

Hang on...

RIPPP

We're in a MASSIVE flea infestation...

Excuse me a second.

So itchy...

Greenwood is covered in fleas...

I CAN'T DO THIS!

WOMP

I'M SO ITCHY!

Wow. This is bad. Thank goodness I flea-proofed this place already!

What do you think is going on?

I don't know, but it's not good!

The phone won't stop ringing! People are afraid to leave their houses!

This flea infestation is all over town!

Fleas aren't THAT big of a deal! I got lice one time in kindergarten and I didn't have to go to school for a week! Best thing that has ever happened to me.

It IS a big deal. People are going to think this is Mayor Good Boy's fault!

It's true. We need to get out there and help.

We can't go outside like this.

It's time to gear up!

Here. Put these on.

PAT PAT PAT

Why do you want us to wear dog collars?

Oh my gosh! Mayor Good Boy! You're so smart!

These are flea collars! They're like anti-flea force fields!

We're gonna look so cool!

HMMM?

Why are these so hard to put on? Man.

Why is Aaron like this?

I ask myself that every day...

So what's the plan?

The plan is to get enough of these collars to everyone in town while we try to get an exterminator out here.

It's weird 'cause the town exterminator isn't answering his phone. Like the one time we really need him!

Wow. That is weird...

So I guess this is where we part ways?

Good luck, dudes! You got this!

You too!

Text me!

You got it!

Let's DO this.

Where did you learn to run so fast?

Do you want to know my secret weapon?

Is your secret weapon candy?

MY SECRET WEAPON IS CANDY!

Nice.

Hang on a second.

I just want to make sure we're going in the right direction.

Uh... Ms. Monica?

Aaron, give me a second, okay?

Aaron...

TAP TAP

I SAID STOP THE TRUCK!

SCREEEEEEEECH

GREENWOOD EXTERMINATORS

Well, looks like we found the exterminators again!

Uhh...

Hey! It's YOU!

BORK BORK BORK

ABANDON SHIP!

GO GO GO!

Abby!
Wait!

C'mon!
They're getting
away!

Let them go.
At least we know
what's going on
now.

Wait...
do we?

Looks like Old
Man Mervis released
all the fleas himself.
I cannot believe I didn't
think of that! He's worked
at the pest control
company for like one
hundred years!

Abby...
are you okay?

I feel like
I'm forgetting
something?

...

Oh man,
I forgot to text
Ms. Monica!

Wait a second.
Have you seen my
phone?

BUZZ
BUZZ

10 MISSED
CALLS

BUZZ

Looks like we have visitors.

♪

Listen up! I know this is going to sound weird, but I need everyone to put on one of these dog collars!

Abby!
Mayor Good Boy!

I think this is how it's supposed to go on?

Oh, wow. We look so tough now!

Stand still, Edward!

A little while later...

You could use one, too.

YES! THIS RULES!

This one might be a little big for you, Aaron.

No way. This is perfect!

Okay, everybody. First off, I want to say I love everyone's fashion choices.

HA HA HA HA HA HA HA HA

I don't get it.

SHHH

We're gonna need some help passing out the rest of these collars around town!

Later that night...

Wait a second... You never told me what happened with the exterminators!

OH MY GOSH! I can't believe we forgot to tell you!

You know that old guy?

Dad?

Hahaha...no. The other old guy... Old Man Mervis!

Oh no! Did he KILL THE EXTERMINATORS?

Wait, what? Kill? Aaron, can you just let me finish my story?

Go on.

So anyways... Old Man Mervis IS an exterminator.

Whaaaa?

It was an inside job! Just like in the movies! The exterminators released all the fleas in town!

Wow.

I knew that guy was trouble from the start!

Why would he do that, though?

BECAUSE GREENWOOD DESERVES BETTER!

Yeah, I unleashed the fleas!

I needed to show this town what would REALLY happen if a dog took over.

Got ya.

What's so funny, huh?

I don't know... It's just that I lost my phone earlier...

What are you going on about? Why should I care about your stupid phone?

Well, a good neighbor found my phone and gave it back to me.

AND?

And I just livestreamed you admitting that you released the fleas in town.

The whole town is watching, Mr. Mervis.

Let's go! We can't let him get away again!

Look up.

Oh man, this is gonna be good!

The next morning...

Citizens of Greenwood, are you itching for a little relief from these past couple of days? If you were affected by the recent flea infestation, you won't want to miss this. Come to the Greenwood Park Pool for a special kind of pool party.

-MAYOR GOOD BOY

Will this itch ever go away?

I'M STILL SO ITCHY!

Thank you for coming, everyone! Trust me, I think you're gonna love what Mayor Good Boy has planned for you!

Aaron, do you copy? The eagle has landed. Over.

Roger. This is Aaron Ableman. We're ready. Over.

OATMEAL POOL PARTY!

Cannonball!

Woooo!

Mayor Good Boy rules!

What a great idea!

Dude, don't eat the oatmeal! Gross!

I'm gonna get ya!

HA HA HA

HA HA HA HA HA HA HA

Mayor Good Boy...can I ask you a question?

Of course, Abby. What is it?

It's just...

Come on, you can tell me anything. That's what friends are for, right?

I'm just wondering, like...of all the people who you could have hired to help you...

Why did I pick you and Aaron?

Yeah... What's so special about us?

The first time I saw you guys...you have no idea how scared I was that day!

Suddenly, I was in charge of an entire town! I thought I was ready, but...

I still get so scared and nervous... even though I'm supposed to be Mayor Good Boy!

You and your brother didn't even know me and wanted to help! You just jumped in and did the right thing!

The world can really use more people like you and your brother.

The town of Greenwood...

The sweetest little place on earth...

Each and every person has a story.

Some have grown up here, and some have just planted their seeds.

But for some, the town has changed.

A once-sleepy community has made national news all because of one little dog.

M. GOOD BOY

PSST. MAYOR GOOD BOY!

M. GOOD BOY

DUDE, WAKE UP!

M. GOOD BOY

Uhhh...

So...

Just because you're a kid doesn't mean you can't change the world!

I used to think that I had to wait till I was older to make a difference...

But then I realized that even the smallest things could make the world a little better!

Go out there and help someone! Anyone!

Wow, Abby. You sound like you have it all figured out!

Like, look at my little brother. He's literally the grossest person I've ever met. One time he ate a hot dog that fell into the pool!

It was only underwater for a few minutes! What's the big deal?

If you'll excuse me...we have something to do...

If Aaron can help someone, so can you!

It's true!

HOW to DRAW MAYOR GOOD BOY

① Draw a circle.

② Now draw two more circles!

③ Add two triangles and a backward "C."

④ Add 5 sticks. (These will be the legs.)

⑤ Make those sticks into feet! (See?)

⑥ Add his face and nose!

202

7 Add a spiral to his tail and some lines to make toes.

8 Now erase a few lines to make things more clear.

9 Add details! Fluff! Collar! His tongue!

10 Don't forget to add color!

And there you have it.
Look at Mayor Good Boy go!

HOW to DRAW
Aaron Ableman!

① Draw a bean.

② Add a long tube for his torso.

③ Add four lines attached to the tube.

④ Add feet to the lines! They're his legs!

⑤ Add two arms.

⑥ Now add two hands!

7 Give him an ear, and start drawing his hair.

8 Add more hair.

9 Add even more hair!

10 Add two circles for eyes.

11 Add Aaron's face and shoelaces.

12 Add color, and you're done! That's Aaron!

HOW to DRAW
Abby Ableman

① Draw a circle. That's Abby's head!

② Add a cone under the circle.

③ Add three lines under the cone.

④ Draw her skirt, and turn the lines into legs!

⑤ Add two arms.

⑥ Add two hands.

7 Add Abby's pigtails.

8 Add two circles for her glasses.

9 Now we'll add some details: her face, eyes, and glasses.

10 Add the top part of Abby's hair here.

11 Then there's the last details: her ears, bow, jacket, and boots!

12 Just add color, and you're done!

The Mayor Good Boy Pledge

I will use my bark more than my bite.

I will try to fart less than a hundred times a week.

I will use my voice to speak for the voiceless.

I will help make my community a better place, one day at a time.

I will never give up, even when times are hard.

I will remember that being different is what makes me special.

I will remember that positive change takes time,
but it's worth fighting for.

I will always root for the underdog.

DAVE SCHEIDT is a writer from Chicago. When he's not writing comic books, he likes watching monster movies and eating snacks. He first started writing stories when he was ten years old and hasn't stopped since.

davescheidt.com

DAVE THANKS

I would first like to thank my family for all the years of support. My father, Thomas Scheidt, who was literally the first person on earth to read my stories and sacrificed everything to help me find my voice. My late mother, Elizabeth Scheidt, was one of the toughest people I have ever met. She had so much love to give even at the very end, and I miss her every day. To my brother, Eric, who filled my life with comic books and toys that shaped me and who supported my creativity since the very beginning. To my sister, Sarah, who has been with me during my darkest days and never gave up on me and made sure I turned out okay. I love you all deeply, and without you this book wouldn't exist.

I would also like to thank Natalie Djordjevic for always believing in me and for the thankless work you have done for my career. I would be lost without you, and I'm so glad to have you in my life. The amount of love and wisdom and laughs you bring is immeasurable. Love you forever and ever.

Thank you to everyone at Random House (Whitney, Gina, Patrick, Nicole) who believed in our little doggie and saw that his story was worth telling. I'd also like to thank Charlie Olsen, Scoot McMahon, Yehudi Mercado, Whitney Gardener, Joey Weiser, Kayla Miller, Steenz and Keya, Ryan, Carrie and Kirby Browne, Josephine M. Yales, Patrick Brower, Nick and Selene Idell, Art Baltazar, Franco Aureliani, Mitch Gerards, Jess Smart Smiley, Kenny Porter, Kris Erickson, Alejandro Rosado, John and Aneta Baran, Tim Beard, Tara Kurtzhals, Tara O'Connor, Andrea Colvin, Hazel Newlevant, Brandon Snider, Trevor Henderson, James Zespy, Shawna Gore, Eric Roesner, Raphael Espinoza, Mike Costa, Andrew Rostan, Rachel Roberts, Bethany Bryan, Elizabeth Brei, Brian Level, Andy Eschenbach, Liz Kozik, Steve Seeley, Jenny Frison, Brian Crowley, Sean Dove, Tony Blando, Jen Sabella, Robert Wilson IV, Tini Howard, Elio, Christopher Sebela, RJ Casey, and everyone and anyone who has supported me throughout the years.

I'd also like to thank each and every librarian, educator, and bookseller who is out there helping kids find themselves in the pages of a book. You are so important, and I'm so grateful to work in an industry with great people like you.

Last but not least, I would like to send all my love to Miranda Harmon. Without her incredibly sweet and beautiful cartooning, this book wouldn't exist. She has brought this book to life in a way I could have never imagined. I am in awe of her creativity, talent, and hard work, and it's been an honor creating this world with her.

MIRANDA HARMON

grew up in Florida and now lives in Los Angeles, where she works and takes care of several houseplants. She graduated from Goucher College and studied comics at the Sequential Artists Workshop. Even though she grew up with cats, she loves dogs too.

🐦 @MirandaMHarmon
mirandaharmon.com

MIRANDA THANKS

First of all, I'd like to thank my parents for being so supportive from the other side of the country. I love and miss you both. Thank you to Tom Hart, Leela Corman, and everyone else at the Sequential Artists Workshop in Gainesville, Florida, for their guidance and kindness. I might not be making books now if I hadn't been given use of the SAW Risograph machine for two years. To my comics friends, you all have changed the course of my life for the better. Thank you for all the convention memories and for helping me navigate this world. Thank you to my agent, Charlie, and to Dave, Whitney, Gina, Patrick, and everyone at Random House for helping this book become something very special. I feel lucky to be a part of this team. Thank you, Reed and Sarah, for your help flatting the book. And thank you to Eric for helping me stay grounded when things get shaky. I love you very much.

DON'T MISS A SINGLE ★ MAYOR ★ GOOD BOY ADVENTURE!

FiND YOUR VOICE
WITH ONE OF THESE EXCITING GRAPHIC NOVELS

PRESENTED BY RH GRAPHIC

f ⊙ @RHKiDSGRAPHiC

A GRAPHIC NOVEL ON EVERY BOOKSHELF